THIS CANDLEWICK BOOK BELONGS TO:

_____

_____

_____

_____

For Mom and Dad and Simon

With thanks to Paddington Pooka
for her example and assistance

Copyright © 1988 by Penny Dale

First U.S. paperback edition 1994
First published in Great Britain in 1988 by Walker Books Ltd., London.

Library of Congress Cataloging-in-Publication Data

Dale, Penny.
Wake up, Mr. B.! / by Penny Dale.—2nd U.S. ed.
Summary: Waking up far too early for her sleepy family, Rosie finds the
family dog Mr. B. is a willing companion for her crack-of-dawn imaginary adventures.
ISBN 1-56402-104-1 (hardcover)—1-56402-382-6 (paperback)
[1. Dogs—Fiction.   2. Imagination—Fiction.   3. Play—Fiction.]
I. Title.   II. Title: Wake up, Mister B.!
PZ7.D1525Wak   1992
[E]—dc20   91-58763

2 4 6 8 10 9 7 5 3 1

Printed in Hong Kong

The pictures in this book were done in ink, watercolor, and crayon.

Candlewick Press
2067 Massachusetts Avenue
Cambridge, Massachusetts 02140

Wake Up,
Mr. B.!

Penny Dale

CANDLEWICK PRESS
CAMBRIDGE, MASSACHUSETTS

Rosie woke up very early.

She went to wake up Billy.

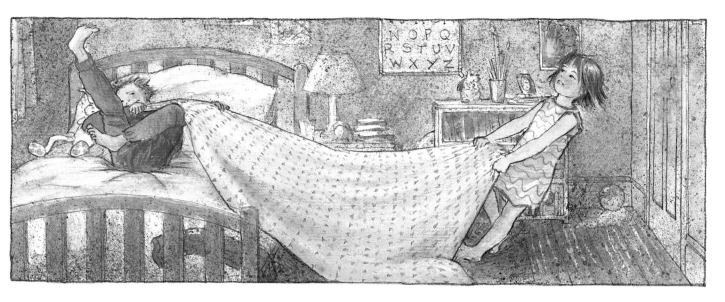

She went to wake up Dad.

She went to find Mr. B.

"Wake up, Mr. B.," she said.

"Come with me, Mr. B.," she said.

"Let's get dressed."

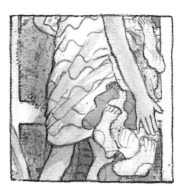

"Get in my car, Mr. B.," she said.

"We're driving to the sea."

"Get in my boat, Mr. B.," she said.

"We're sailing around the world."

"Get in my balloon, Mr. B.," she said.

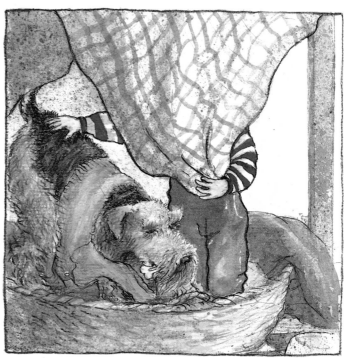

"Don't fall asleep. We're flying to the moon."

"Come and see Rosie and Mr. B.," said Billy.

"Wake up, Rosie! Wake up, Mr. B.!"

PENNY DALE began her picture book using "many, many words," but it eventually became "a nearly wordless book." She explains, "I felt that the book still needed some words to act as a skeleton, to guide the reader through." Penny Dale is also the author and illustrator of *Ten Out of Bed* and *All About Alice*.